17⁹⁹

D0771417

To Donovan,
for being random, having conviction,
and making sense of it all
—J. E. J.

For Pierre
—S. C.

SIMON & SCHUSTER BOOKS FOR YOUNG READERS
An imprint of Simon & Schuster Children's Publishing Division
1230 Avenue of the Americas, New York, New York 10020
Text copyright © 2020 by Jonathan E. Jacobs
Illustrations copyright © 2020 by Samantha Cotterill
SIMON & SCHUSTER BOOKS FOR YOUNG READERS is a trademark of Simon & Schuster, Inc.
For information about special discounts for bulk purchases, please contact Simon & Schuster Special
Sales at 1-866-506-1949 or business@simonandschuster.com.
The Simon & Schuster Speakers Bureau can bring authors to your live event. For more information or
to book an event, contact the Simon & Schuster Speakers Bureau
at 1-866-248-3049 or visit our website at www.simonspeakers.com.
Book design by Lizzy Bromley · The text for this book was set in Colby.
The illustrations for this book are hand-built three-dimensional sets containing digitally colored
hand-drawn pieces (with nib pen and ink) cut and assembled, painted cardboard, and the cutest
miniature lightbulb shot with a digital SLR camera.
Manufactured in China · 0220 SCP · First Edition
2 4 6 8 10 9 7 5 3 1
Library of Congress Cataloging-in-Publication Data
Names: Jacobs, Jonathan E., author. | Cotterill, Samantha, illustrator.
Title: The secret rhino society / written by Jonathan E. Jacobs ; illustrated by Samantha Cotterill.
Description: First edition. | New York : Simon & Schuster Books for Young Readers, [2020] | "A Paula
Wiseman Book." | Audience: Ages 4–8. | Audience: Grades 2-3. | Summary: "A hippo, a worm, and a
lightbulb form a club to celebrate their favorite animal, the rhinoceros. But when the trio actually
meets a rhino, they are disappointed to find she is not what they expected"—Provided by publisher.
Identifiers: LCCN 2019028106 (print) | LCCN 2019028107 (eBook) |
ISBN 9781534430006 (hardcover) | ISBN 9781534430013 (eBook)
Subjects: CYAC: Clubs—Fiction. | Friendship—Fiction. | Rhinocerous—Fiction. | Humorous stories.
Classification: LCC PZ7.1.J37 Sec 2020 (print) | LCC PZ7.1.J37 (eBook) | DDC [E]—dc23
LC record available at https://lccn.loc.gov/2019028106

THE SECRET RHINO SOCIETY

written by
JONATHAN E.
JACOBS

illustrated by
SAMANTHA
COTTERILL

A Paula Wiseman Book
Simon & Schuster Books for Young Readers
New York London Toronto Sydney New Delhi

Fran, Hudson, and Jean
had one thing in common.
Each of them wanted to be . . .

a rhinoceros.

Hudson loved how fast they could charge.

Fran loved how intimidating they were.

Jean was especially fond of their unbreakable horns.

So the three friends formed
a secret society. Their first order of
business was to build a clubhouse
where they could meet up and
admire their favorite animal.

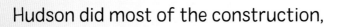

Hudson did most of the construction,

Fran prepared the dirt
for the garden,

and Jean
provided light
when they
worked into
the night.

Or ate
sandwiches
together.

When the clubhouse was complete, they called it the "Rhinocer-House".

They made themselves paper horns so that they could look and feel more like rhinoceroses.

Some horns fit better than others.

THUD!

Hudson led the meetings. Fran wrote the meeting notes with mud. And Jean kept things bright, while doing their best not to catch their paper horn on fire.

Although
sometimes this
happened.

They were a little embarrassed that they were wearing paper horns, so Hudson called out: "This is a private club! I'm afraid there isn't room for any other members. Another time, perhaps."

But the knocking continued, and when the clubhouse began to shake, he opened the door. It was ...

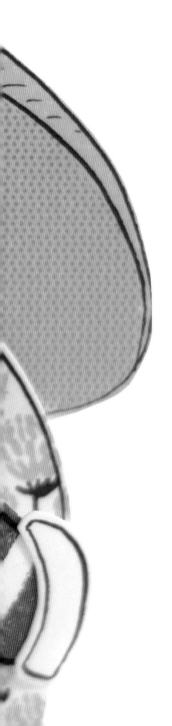

a rhinoceros!

"Which one of you is Fran? Can you sign here,
please?" asked the rhinoceros.
"What . . . what . . . why are you . . . why are
you wearing that outfit?!" stammered Hudson.

"This is what I always wear!" declared the rhinoceros, who said her name was Ivy.
"I have your delivery."

"Before you go,"
asked Hudson,
"can't you show us

how to charge . . .

or snort . . .

or sharpen our horns?"

"I'm a gardener," Ivy replied. "I work at a garden store and deliver plants!"

"Did I get your order wrong?" she asked anxiously.
"No," replied Hudson. "You . . . you are just not
what we expected a rhinoceros to be."

"I'm sorry you're disappointed," said Ivy.
"Anyway, you folks are going to have a really
beautiful garden."

Imagining how hungry she must be after a long day of work, the friends invited the rhinoceros to stay for cheese and pickle sandwiches.

As they ate, Ivy shared gardening stories and soaked her hooves in a soothing mud mixture specially prepared by Fran.

"I'm having such a wonderful time," offered Ivy. "Have you ever thought of opening your own sandwich shop?"

The friends agreed that what they loved most about having a secret society was making and sharing sandwiches. They wondered what it might it be like to invite others along. So . . .

they got to work!

Hudson put together
the sandwich menu.

Fran perfected several
new mud recipes.

Jean played with
mood lighting.

And Ivy did the landscaping.

The next week, they opened their new sandwich shop.

And everyone came.